DAVE

THE LONELY MONSTER

Anna Kemp and Sara Ogilvie

SIMON & SCHUSTER

London   New York   Sydney   Toronto   New Delhi

Once upon a time, in a retirement cave,
Lived a lonely monster. His name was DAVE.

In his bad old days, he'd been a pest,

He'd romped,

he'd roared,

he'd made a mess,

Till folks who like things nice and neat,
And don't like monsters on their street,

Banished Dave to Echo Rock,
Lonesome as a single sock.

Poor Dave!

And there he stayed for six decades,
Just Dave and his guitar,

Strumming songs no one could hear,
From dusk to the morning star.

And, even worse, the local knights
Would try to get old Dave to fight
By laughing at his toothy grin,
His wonky ears and scaly skin.

But Dave would never harm a flea,
He's not the fighting sort, you see,

He'd rather play some rock and roll

Or take a bath, to soothe the soul.

Then one day, as old Dave dozed,
A cabbage bopped him on the nose,

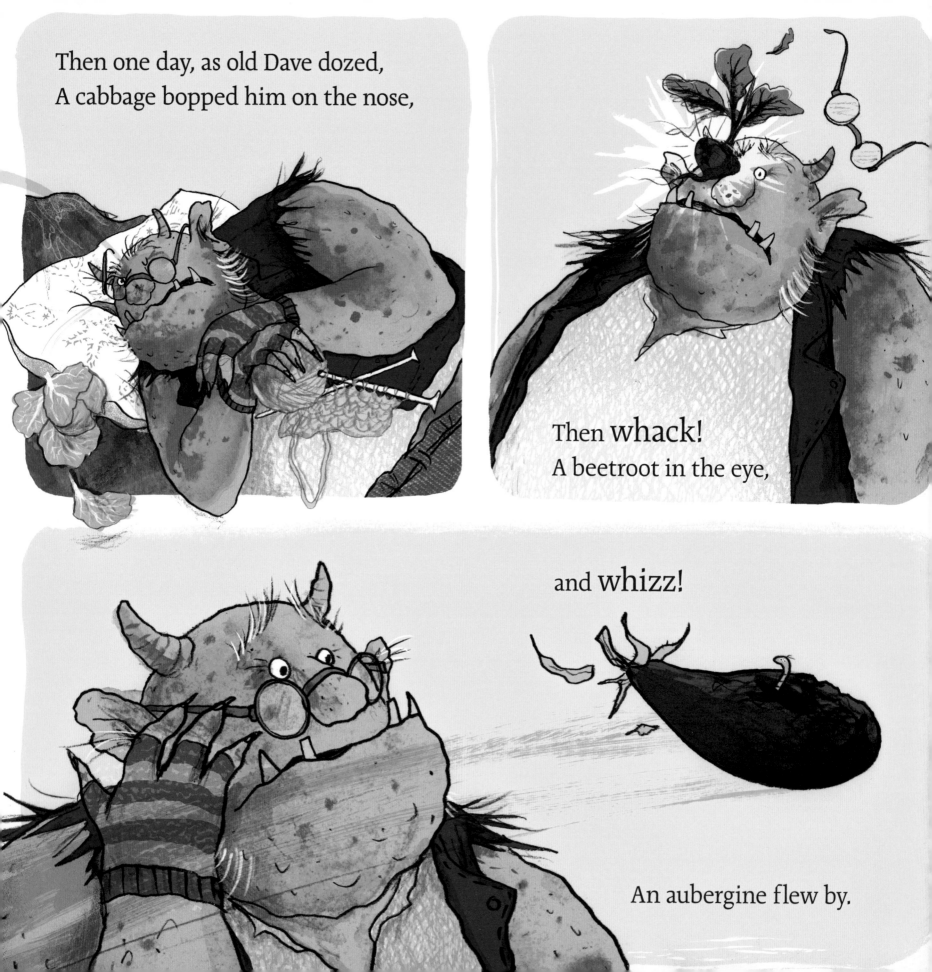

Then whack!
A beetroot in the eye,

and whizz!

An aubergine flew by.

Then leaping from behind the gorse,
A tiny knight, on a hobby horse,
Waved a carrot at the sky,

"Prepare to meet your **doom!**" he cried.

"How old are you?" the monster gasped.
"I'm six," said tiny, "since you asked.

My name is Percival the Brave,
And you're that fiendish monster, Dave!"

The monster rubbed his aching head,
"Well that's not very nice," he said.
"Don't you know a proper knight
Is always kindly and polite?

And though I might look fierce to you,
We monstrous beasts have feelings too."

Percy hadn't thought of that,
He stopped and stared, subdued,

Then blushed down to his boots and said,

"I'm sorry I was rude."

So Percy took a knightly pledge
To give up throwing rotten veg,
And by the time the week had ended . . .

. . . knight and beast were best-befriended.

They shared a taste
in monster rock,

Took a spin
around the block,

Watched the jousting on TV,

At last,
old Dave had company!

But back in town, across the bay,
Folks got grumpier by the day.

Tranquility had reigned for years,
And everyone was bored to tears.

They sighed, "You know what would be smashing?
A good old-fashioned monster-bashing!

Why don't we make a day of it?
Now that should perk us up a bit."

And so they grabbed some mushy fruits,
Some rotten veg and mouldy roots,

And headed out to Echo Rock,
Where Dave was knitting winter socks.

Then just as they were taking aim,

A furious knight with eyes aflame,
Came charging through the swelling crowd,

"Knock it off!" he cried aloud.

"What's this nonsense! Can't you behave?
Is that any way to treat old Dave?

He may rock out from time to time
But is that such a dreadful crime?

Now chuck out those potato peelings,
And spare a thought for old Dave's feelings!"

The townsfolk all felt mighty humbled,
"We didn't mean it, Dave," they mumbled.

Dave smiled and shook his massive head,
"If you really want some fun," he said,
"Then put away the salad bar
And let me fetch my bass guitar!"

And so they went down to the cave . . .

. . . and had themselves a monster rave.

They danced and sang and danced some more,
Bust some moves on Dave's dance floor,

Had a riot, learned to jive,

And got more MONSTER in their lives.

So old Dave got his groove back on,
And was alone no more,

Thanks to a fiercely gentle knight
Who knew that he would rather fight . . .

. . . For love and peace,
not war.

For Cleo and Esme, and their
wonderful mum and dad – AK

For Johanna and Alics – SO

SIMON & SCHUSTER

First published in Great Britain in 2018 by Simon & Schuster UK Ltd
1st Floor, 222 Gray's Inn Road, London, WC1X 8HB • A CBS Company • Text copyright
© 2018 Anna Kemp • Illustrations copyright © 2018 Sara Ogilvie • The right of Anna
Kemp and Sara Ogilvie to be identified as the author and illustrator of this work has
been asserted by them in accordance with the Copyright, Designs and Patents Act, 1988
All rights reserved, including the right of reproduction in whole or in part in any form
A CIP catalogue record for this book is available from the British Library upon request
978-1-4711-4367-0 (HB) • 978-1-4711-4368-7 (PB) • 978-1-4711-4369-4 (eBook)
Printed in China • 10 9 8 7 6 5 4 3 2 1

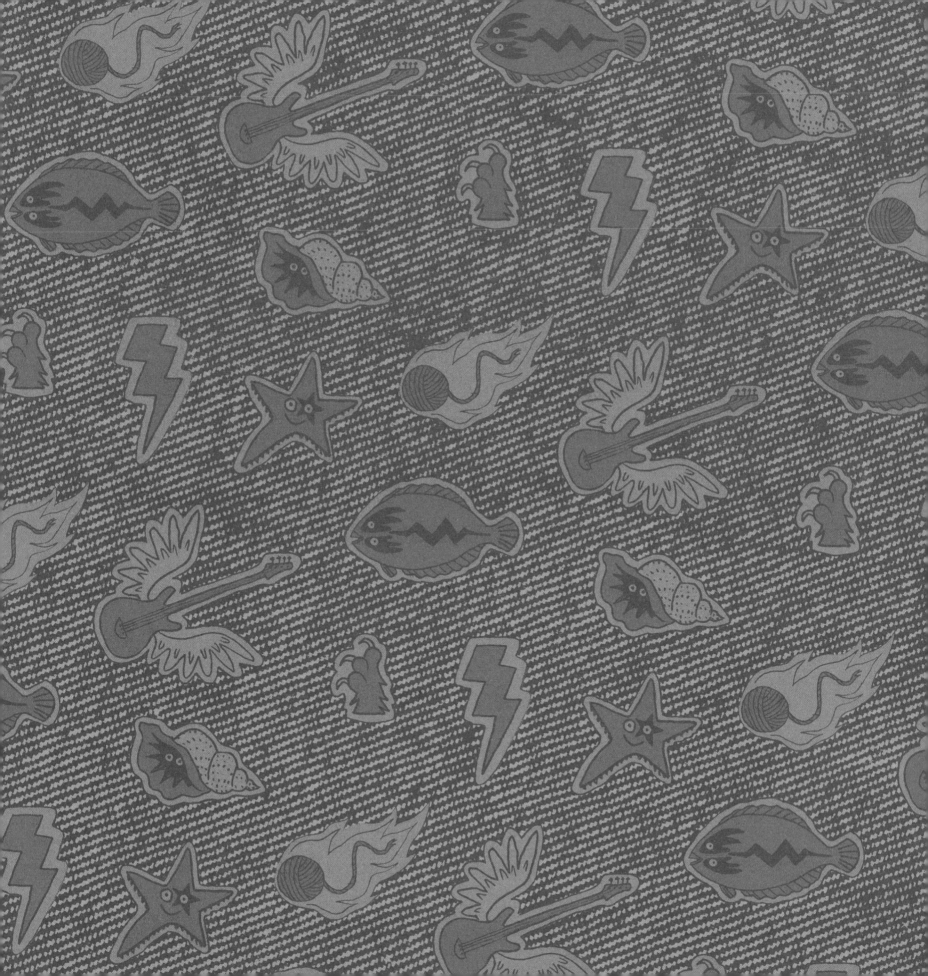